Peppa introduced Suzy to her toy horse. "Suzy, meet
Horsey Twinkle Toes. Horsey Twinkle Toes, meet Suzy."
"It's very nice to meet you, Miss Twinkle Toes,"
said Suzy politely.

Peppa and Suzy galloped off to Peppa's bedroom together.
"Giddy-up, Horsey!" shouted Peppa, racing around her room on Horsey Twinkle Toes while Suzy watched.

Thud!

Thud!

My magical unicorn's name is

. . . .

LADYBIRD BOOKS

UK | USA | Canada | Ireland | Australia | India | New Zealand | South Africa

Ladybird Books is part of the Penguin Random House group of companies
whose addresses can be found at global.penguinrandomhouse.com.

www.penguin.co.uk   www.puffin.co.uk   www.ladybird.co.uk

First published 2018
008

Printed in China

A CIP catalogue record for this book is available from the British Library

ISBN: 978-0-241-35378-3

All correspondence to:
Ladybird Books
Penguin Random House Children's
80 Strand, London WC2R 0RL

MIX
Paper from
responsible sources
FSC
www.fsc.org
FSC® C018179

Peppa's ✦ Magical ✦ Unicorn

One rainy day, Peppa invited Suzy Sheep
to her house to play.
"Hello, Suzy," cried Peppa, when she arrived.
"Let's play with my horse!"

Daddy Pig heard all the noise and came upstairs
to see what was going on.
"We're playing horses!" cried Peppa.
"I see," said Daddy Pig, seeing Suzy sitting quietly.

"Do you think perhaps it's Suzy's turn, Peppa?" asked Daddy Pig.
"Yes," replied Peppa. "Come on, Suzy. You can ride
Horsey Twinkle Toes now."
"I don't want to play horses," sighed Suzy. "I want to play unicorns."

Peppa thought for a moment. "Well, Horsey Twinkle Toes is
a magic horse," she said. "She can be a unicorn whenever
she feels like it."

"Oh," said Suzy. "OK."

Suzy pranced around the room on Horsey Twinkle Toes.
"Let's brush her beautiful tail," said Peppa.
"But unicorns have rainbow tails," said Suzy.

"Oh," said Peppa. "That's OK.
We can put coloured ribbons in it!"
"What a good idea," said Daddy Pig.
"You do that, while I get you
both a snack."

"Now we can fly in the sky on our unicorn!" cheered Peppa.
"But a unicorn has a horn to hold when you fly," said Suzy.
"Horsey Twinkle Toes doesn't have a horn."
"Oh," said Peppa. "That's OK. She flies so gently,
you don't even have to hold on!"

Peppa and Suzy took it in turns to fly around the room.
"I wish Horsey Twinkle Toes was a real unicorn," said Suzy.
"And I wish she was really, really, really sparkly!" added Peppa.
"I think Horsey Twinkle Toes is tired," said Daddy Pig.
"Why don't you build her a den to sleep in?"
"Yay!" cheered Peppa and Suzy.

While Peppa and Suzy were busy building a den in the living room, Daddy Pig gathered some secret supplies for later. "Wow," said Daddy Pig, when Peppa and Suzy had finished. "What a fantastic den!"

"Can we sleep in it tonight, Daddy?" asked Peppa. "Pleeeeease!"
"Of course," said Daddy Pig. "If Mummy Sheep says it's OK,
you can have a sleepover in the den."
"Hooray!" cheered Peppa and Suzy.

After dinner, Peppa and Suzy got ready for their sleepover.
"Please can you read us a bedtime story
all about unicorns, Daddy?" asked Peppa.
"Of course," Daddy Pig replied.

When the story was finished,
Peppa and Suzy snuggled up in
their cosy den and fell fast asleep.

While Peppa and Suzy slept,
Daddy Pig picked up Horsey Twinkle Toes,
tiptoed outside and quietly set to work painting . . .

And painting some more . . .

Then sticking . . .

And sticking some more . . .

And then, Daddy Pig added the final touch . . .
. . . A HORN!
Daddy Pig sneaked back to the den
to return Horsey Twinkle Toes.
"Ta-da!" he whispered.

Then he went upstairs, and was about to go to sleep when he heard . . .

"Wow!"

Peppa and Suzy gasped loudly.

They had woken up to find that Horsey Twinkle Toes
had transformed into a magical unicorn.
"I told you Horsey Twinkle Toes was magic!" said Peppa.
"She's perfect!" added Suzy.

The next morning, Peppa, Suzy, George, Mummy and Daddy Pig all sat down for breakfast.

Peppa told her family what had happened.

"And, when we woke up, Horsey Twinkle Toes had turned into a real unicorn!" gasped Peppa. "It's magic!"

"Hmmm," said Daddy Pig sleepily.

"How wonderful!" said Mummy Pig. "It sounds like you and Suzy have had the perfect sleepover."
"Yes!" said Peppa. "But why does Daddy have paint all over his face?"
Daddy Pig couldn't answer. He had fallen asleep at the table!

After breakfast, Peppa and Suzy headed off
on a magical adventure with their new unicorn.
"I love your magical unicorn!" cheered Suzy.
"Me too!" said Peppa.
Everyone loves magical unicorns!